Window

Jeannie Baker

I am grateful to Haydn Washington, biologist
and environmental writer and consultant, for his help.

The artwork was prepared as collage constructions which were reproduced in full colour from photographs by David Cummings. The cover art was photographed by Murray Van Der Veer.
The words have been typeset in Garamond.

Find out more about Jeannie Baker's books by visiting her website at www.jeanniebaker.com

This edition published 2002
by Walker Books Ltd
87 Vauxhall Walk, London SE11 5HJ

20 19 18 17 16

Printed in China

British Library Cataloguing in Publication Data:
a catalogue record for this book is available from the British Library

ISBN 978-0-7445-9486-7

www.walker.co.uk

To Rodney, Haydn and David

2
Birthday
ou are 2
xxx

FRAGILE
Happy Birthday
today you are

Happy

Happy
Birthday

DELI
CUPS
delight your day
ORDERS

FOR SALE
NO BREAD

MKK 555

FIRE
WOOD
SOLD
HERE
THE FORT

FIRE
WOOD
SOLD

HAPPY 16th Birthday

Science
Homework

'Its only a bottle top'
GARBAGE!
CIG
BUTTS?
McDonalds
circus

BRIAN WESTLAKE
CARES
BURGER

McDonalds

SIMPS
Save here
PIZZA
1.99
PECIAL
KED BEANS
MOUTH
ave a
ful Day!
love
Tracy X

McDonalds
KEEP OFF
THE GRASS
REMOVALS
BROWNS
Ph 02 - 8101771
HIY210

PIZZA
Enjoy
Coke
TAKE AWAY FOOD
CHOC
ICECREAM
tub
65c
PEELED
TOMATOES
45c
$1.99

House Blocks
FOR SALE
24
TODAY

AUTHOR'S NOTE

In this book I set out to tell the complicated issue of how we are changing the environment without knowing it. This change is hard to see from day to day but it is nevertheless happening and it is happening fast.

The facts are alarming. Scientists estimate that if we continue to destroy wilderness at this pace, by the year 2020 no wilderness will remain on our planet except for land protected in national parks and reserves.

By the same year, they estimate a quarter of our plant and animal species will be extinct.

Already, at least two species become extinct each hour.

But by opening a window in our minds, by understanding how change takes place and by changing the way we personally affect the environment, we can make a difference.

JEANNIE BAKER was born in England and now lives in Australia. The collage constructions in her books are also designed as exhibitions. They have been exhibited in galleries in London, New York and throughout Australia and are part of many public art collections. She is the author-artist of a number of distinguished picture books including: *Home in the Sky*, an ALA Notable Book, Commended Australian Children's Picture Book of the Year; *Where the Forest Meets the Sea*, IBBY Honour Award, Friends of the Earth Earthworm Award; *The Hidden Forest*, Australian Wilderness Society Fiction Award; and *The Story of Rosy Dock*, an ALA Notable Book and Australian Picture Book of the Year Honour Book.

THE PICTURES in this book are photographs of collages. "I started," says Jeannie Baker, "by making drawings of my ideas on paper and collecting grasses, vegetation, tree bark, earth, fabric for clothing and any other materials that I thought would work in these pictures. I treated the natural materials to preserve them and added my own colour. The original collages are miniatures ... the same size as reproduced in this book."